RUDI
AND THE DISTELFINK

By F. N. Monjo. Pictures by George Kraus

Windmill Books, Inc.
and E. P. Dutton & Co., Inc.
New York

23215
NORTON PUBLIC LIBRARY
101 E. LINCOLN
NORTON, KANSAS 67654

Text copyright © 1972, by F. N. Monjo
Illustrations copyright © 1972, by George Kraus

All rights reserved.

Published simultaneously in Canada by
Clarke, Irwin & Company Limited,
Toronto and Vancouver

SBN: 0-525-61002-2   LCC: 72-86275

Printed in the U.S.A.
First Edition

To My Grandsons
Ivan and Andrew

George Kraus

The Family

JANUARY

On our farm, first of all, there's me, Rudi Schimmelpfennig. Then there's my Vati—that's for Papa, in Pennsylvania Dutch, ja? And my Mutti, Mama. And Mutti's Mama Grossmutter Ritter—like you say, my granny. And plenty kinder. That's us Schimmelpfennig children. I mean you'd *think* there's plenty, except for what Mutti says.

"Ach! Eli Schimmelpfennig!" says Mutti. "How do you expect a woman should do all I got to do on this farm, with only three daughters to help? Only Anna-Marie, and Daisy, and Lena . . ."

"Liebchen," says Vati to Mutti, "maybe someday we still have some more daughters. But, for now, you got eight boys and three girls to help you, ain't?"

"Eli Schimmelpfennig!" says Mutti. "Do boys spin flax and card wool? Do boys do the weaving? Or make the soap? Or dip the candles? Or churn butter. Or . . ."

"Liebchen! Liebchen!" laughs Vati. "It's not such a small family. Gives Eli. And Pete. And Stevie. And the twins, Yonni and Yonkel. And Rudi. And Bernie. And Moe. And Anna-Marie. And Daisy. And Lena. And still you got to complain?"

"And what about Anna-Marie?" says Mutti. "Ain't she going skating tonight on the millpond with Willi Stolzfuss? Ain't she big enough to be married, maybe, before long?"

FEBRUARY

That Anna-Marie! Always sewing sheets and towels for her wedding chest. With colors embroidered—red pomegranates, orange tulips, pink roses, white and yellow daisies, and green and blue peacocks. And on everything, almost, she sews the distelfink (he's that little yellow bird, with the crest on his head, that Mutti says is for luck and happiness).

The lambs get born in February. Sometimes, late at night, Vati wakes me up and he and Eli and Pete and Stevie and I go out to the barn to help the sheep. Vati lets me hold the lamp.

Late this month on the coldest nights the sap in the sugar maples begins to run. Then we collect the sugar water from the trees and it's boiled and boiled, to make maple syrup.

One night when we're out skating, Moe falls through the ice, and Bernie crawls out to the edge of the hole to fish him out. And Bernie falls in, too! Yonni and Yonkel get a ladder and a pitchfork, and we pull them both out of the water and take them home.

"Dummheit and Firlefanz!" says Mutti. "Stupidity and Nonsense! Now you'll *both* be wonderful sick!"

But Grossmutter Ritter says, "Rudi, run up to the attic, and bring a crock of gensfet. Hurry." Then Mutti and Grossmutter rub Bernie and Moe all over the chest and back with the nice oily goosegrease, and wrap them up in strips of red flannel, and put them to bed with three quilts over. And they don't get sick at all.

MARCH

Spring is coming, and the geese fly up from the south, making V's across the sky.

Mutti says, "Eli Schimmelpfennig! Now that he's going to marry our Anna-Marie, it's time we should have Willi Stolzfuss here for a meal. And it's time for the pastor to call out, for them, in church."

So, next Sunday, all of us get dressed up and drive off to church in our buggies. Pastor Waldensius reads out, real loud, how Anna-Marie Schimmelpfennig and Willi Stolzfuss want to get married, and why should anybody want to stop them? Mutti and Grossmutter wipe their eyes on handkerchiefs. And then all the Stolzfuss family come back to our house for a big dinner. It's baked ham and a roast leg of lamb and potatoes and gravy and turnips and snitz pie and custard pie and everything.

Willi's father gives Anna-Marie a big kiss, and so does Mama Stolzfuss, and everybody at the table smiles and laughs at Willi and Anna-Marie. Then Willi gets red in the face and tramps out on the porch, to cool off, maybe? And he's so big, every step he takes the floor sort of bounces and shakes, and the glassware tinkles on the table.

"Donnerwetter!" says Vati. "I think maybe we scare the poor little weakling!"

And everybody laughs some more.

APRIL

Anna-Marie wants to take our distelfink from the mantelpiece, for her new house, when she marries Willi Stolzfuss. And Mutti says, "Sure, why not?" But what will we do for luck and happiness, when all of it's gone with Anna-Marie?

This month, some of us boys help Vati with the plowing. It smells good when the plow goes through, and the earth turns up all dark and damp and warm. Birds fly down from the fields to eat the worms the plow turns up in the furrows.

Vati tells us that in the old days, when *his* grandfather first came here from Switzerland, the old people always knew where the best rich land was, wherever they found black walnut trees growing! And ain't we got a nice grove of them black walnut trees, right on the Schimmelpfennig farm?

In April you might see some early violets, and some blue Quaker ladies blooming. The cows are out, eating the new grass, with their new calves. And under the willows, the mares are running with their new colts.

Mutti starts thinking about Willi Stolzfuss, and she says, "What will I do without my Anna-Marie and without my little distelfink on the mantelpiece?"

And then she goes to the barnyard to see about her hens. The eggs have hatched at last. All the hens Mutti set got little yellow chicks now running and pecking everywhere. And you know what Grossmutter Ritter says about them hens and chicks? She says, "It's *klooks mit peeps!*"

MAY

Everything in May is blossoms. Here's how they come, first the cherry, then apple, pear, plum, and peach. Cherry is almost all white, with tiny pink spots inside you can't hardly see. Apple is pale pink. Pear is pure white, with inside tiny little green dots. And plum is white with a little red. And peach is the pinkest of them all.

When the apple trees bloom, Grossmutter takes her hives of bees from the shed and sets them out in the orchard. There the bees begin to make their honey from the nectar in the blossoms. Grossmutter says apple honey tastes different from all the other honeys the bees can make. And she can tell them all apart, clover, and buckwheat, and wild honey, too.

May is when Vati and Eli and Pete and Stevie run the sheep through the pond, to wash their fleeces. Then they comb them, and later on they shear them.

When the leaves on the oaks begin to open, Vati starts planting. He puts four grains of corn to a hill. Here's what he says: "One for the worm, one for the crow, one for the rain, and one to grow!"

JUNE

There's thrushes and robins in the cherry trees, eating all they can hold. Soon Yonni and Yonkel and I can climb the trees and pick the fruit. And Mutti will make cherry pies and tarts and preserves.

Wheat and barley are turning golden brown in the fields, and the strawberries are getting ripe.

The roses are blooming. Vati and the big boys cut the hay, and the air smells sweet for days. The cows go down to the brook to eat watercress and mint and clover. They have the sweetest breath in the whole world.

Yonni and Yonkel and I go to the shed to watch Vati and Eli and Stevie and Pete shearing the rams and ewes. Vati knows how to shear off a fleece, all in one piece, just like a rug.

Willi Stolzfuss comes over to our farm to tell us he's got a new job now, driving a big Conestoga freight wagon, with a team of six big horses. You have to be some big strong man to handle six strong horses. Willi says he'll be traveling from Lancaster to Philadelphia and back, and then from Lancaster to York and back, every week.

"Willi Stolzfuss," says Anna-Marie. "You just be careful!"

I keep thinking how sad Mutti will be, when Anna Marie and our distelfink on the mantelpiece go off to live with Willi Stolzfuss, and I think maybe I should do something about it, ja?

JULY

Anna-Marie and Willi Stolzfuss want to get married before Christmas, so I got to get Mutti a new distelfink by then. Willi Stolzfuss says he'll show me how to carve one. He says he'll take me with him to Philadelphia, in his wagon, to buy me some gouges and chisels. And wouldn't I like to go?

Vati hired some extra hands for the wheat harvest. And now Mutti and Grossmutter and the girls have extra big meals to cook for all those extra men. Yonni and Yonkel and me carry out iced drinks for them, in the fields.

Sometimes we slip off to pick raspberries, where they grow, down by the quarry.

Yonni and Yonkel and Bernie and Moe and me like to go swimming in the brook, when we can chase the cows out first. They're wonderful hard to drive out of the cool water. And Grossmutter says, "They need to cool off, too, ain't?"

Then a thunderstorm comes up and pretty soon it's raining and thundering, with flashes of lightning.

"Ach!" says Grossmutter, looking up at the sky. "The Old Man is beating his wife!"

AUGUST

Anna-Marie is saying she don't ever want to marry Willi Stolzfuss, because now she don't want to leave home. Mutti says that's Firlefanz and big nonsense and Dummheit, because every girl should get married, and where could she ever find such a nice young fellow again like Willi Stolzfuss? And so Anna-Marie decides maybe she'll get married, after all.

Willi Stolzfuss and I are going to go to Philadelphia today, in Willi's wagon. As we ride along, I can see the oats in the fields. They've turned from green to yellow to brown, and they'll all be cut and stored in barns before we get back from Philadelphia.

Willi Stolzfuss wants to buy Anna-Marie a present in Philadelphia, for their wedding. I'm going to get some carving tools so I can make Mutti's new distelfink.

As Willi Stolzfuss and I are driving along outside of Lancaster, on every farm we pass we can see them out in the fields, cutting hay, or in the orchard, picking peaches and plums.

Near Downingtown, when we stop to water the horses, farmer Weismuller yells to us his well has gone dry in the heat.

We stay at the inn in Downingtown, and Willi Stolzfuss has a fight with a man who drives in after us, but wants to water his horses first.

"Don't make me mad, you!" says Willi Stolzfuss.

But the man makes Willi Stolzfuss mad, anyway. So Willi has to wrestle him, and the man gets his arm broke! That Willi Stolzfuss is some strong somebody!

Willi Stolzfuss buys me my carving tools in Philadelphia, right after we go to market and unload all our eggs and chickens and cheeses that we brought from the farm. And Willi Stolzfuss buys some red beads and some lace and a gold ring for Anna-Marie.

And while we're driving back next day, I remind Willi Stolzfuss that he must help me carve a new distelfink for Mutti—for good luck and happiness—after Anna-Marie is married with Willi Stolzfuss, and she takes our distelfink away.

I make Willi Stolzfuss promise to keep the whole thing secret, though. Because that distelfink is a surprise. For Christmas. For Mutti.

SEPTEMBER

"Eli Schimmelpfennig," says Mutti to Vati. "There's not enough girls on this place to help with all the work I got! No sir! Now I got pickles to make, and catsup to put up, and grapes to boil for jelly, and more grapes to dry for raisins, and apples and pears coming."

"Same like every year, ain't?" says Vati.

He's working wonderful hard, too. After the oats is cut and stored away in the barn, he has to plow the fields it grew in. And he has to sow it again, this time with winter wheat, for next year.

When it's apple-picking time, we have a big party, and Mutti and all the women and girls sit down at long tables and take the cores out and peel the apples and cut them up in slices. Then they dry the slices in the oven, so that they can keep them up in the attic, on strings, all winter long. That's snitz. Sure! And snitz pie is the best in the whole world!

After the snitz party, Mutti and Grossmutter and the girls have *another* party and they ask all our friends over to the farm. And everybody puts cider in some big copper vats, and when it starts boiling, they throw in some snitz and cinnamon and cloves and sassafras. And that boils and boils some more. And when it gets nice and thick, that's apple butter!

OCTOBER

The air is all blue and smoky and sweet-smelling, over by Ironstone Mountain. The wild geese are flying back south, in V's across the sky.

"Rudi Schimmelpfennig," says Mutti. "You and Yonni and Yonkel go into the woods and bring in the last of the butternuts, and walnuts, and chestnuts."

As we was out, gathering nuts, we saw the squirrels and the chipmunks at work, storing up hickory nuts and seeds for winter. The leaves are as red and orange as they'll ever be. The corn shocks are all bundled in the fields. And there's nothing left to bring in, except squash and pumpkins.

Yesterday, Lena and Daisy found a tree with bittersweet growing up in its branches, and they cut some.

This morning there was a skim of ice on the pond, and the mud puddles was frozen tight.

Anna-Marie and I ain't so much help on the farm this year. Both of us is busy. She's got her wedding dress to finish before Thanksgiving. And I got my distelfink to carve by Christmas.

I got a secret from Mutti that Mutti don't know. It's about the distelfink. But there's more. I ain't carving *one*. I'm carving *two!*

NOVEMBER

Come November, Vati butchers the hogs and we start smoking hams and grinding meat for sausages. Mutti boils up the extra fat in kettles, for soap. Grossmutter kills some of her ducks and geese, and plucks off all their feathers, for stuffing quilts and pillows. Then she roasts the geese, and pours the fat in jars. For goosegrease, for when we fall through the ice *this* winter!

Come Thanksgiving, Anna-Marie and Willi Stolzfuss get married. We have roast goose for the wedding feast. Roast goose with chestnut stuffing and apple butter and smoked ham baked in brown sugar, with spiced apples and honey and watermelon-rind pickle and cauliflower and kale and corn-bread and pickled onions and cucumber pickle and pickalilly and mashed potatoes and gravy. And there's pumpkin pie and raisin pie and snitz pie and custard pie and three kinds of cake for dessert.

"A proper wedding feast," says Pastor Waldensius, and he passes Willi Stolzfuss and Anna-Marie's wedding certificate around the table for everyone to see. So beautiful with flowers and birds painted on it!

Then Willi and Anna-Marie go away together, and some of the grown-ups cry. It begins to snow a little in the late afternoon. Grossmutter says, "Look at that, will you? Early the Old Man starts plucking his geese this year."

DECEMBER

Vati says we all got to be good to Mutti now, until after the baby comes. Ja. Sure! Mutti's going to have another baby. Vati says he hopes it's a girl, so Mutti won't complain no more, about not enough girls. I hope so, too.

Mutti don't take things easy, though. Tomorrow's Christmas Eve, and Mutti and Grossmutter and the girls are all in the kitchen, making keks for Christmas. Cookies!

And under the Christmas tree, in the sitting room, Vati is making a Putz. That's a little scene, with mountains and snow and a Bethlehem town, and Mary and Joseph and the baby Jesus in a manger. And a star.

All at once I hear Mutti holler.

"Donnerwetter!" says Vati. "It's coming now, the baby." And he and Eli carry Mutti up to her bedroom. Then Vati and Pete drive away in the sleigh to fetch Dr. Krankmann.

A half hour after they're gone, "Lieber Gott!" calls Grossmutter. "Daisy! Lena! Come! You wouldn't believe what Mutti done! She went and had some twins already, a *second* time!"

So there is Mutti, in bed, with her two new babies, side by side like two little roses. Two little girls, named Lise and Lotte. Now is the time for my surprise! I give my present to Mutti. She looks at the two distelfinks I carved and she begins to laugh.

"They're for luck and happiness," I say. "And for Lise and Lotte, too."

Then Vati and the big boys and Dr. Krankmann come back in the sleigh. They bring with them also Willi Stolzfuss and Anna-Marie. When everybody sees the twins and the distelfinks I made, Vati smiles at me. And he says to Mutti, "Look what Rudi done for you. Two more girls he brought you."

And Mutti smiles, and says, "Ja. Two!"

Pretty soon Lise and Lotte are sleeping in pink blankets, just as cozy as can be. And Pastor Waldensius comes to the house and paints twin geburtscheins — birth certificates — for them, in beautiful colors.

And Grossmutter says, "Now, Greta, maybe you got enough girls to be satisfied for a while."

"Ja," says Mutti. "Enough boys I had. And now I got enough girls, too. So I'm happy."

And so everything turns out just the way it should. For our family and for every family. When it's Christmas. Ain't?

Geburt u. Taufschein.

Diesen Ehegatten Eli und Greta Schimmelpfennig geb. Kraus sind den 25ten Dez. 1820 im Jahre unseres Herrn die Tochter Lise geboren. In Hummeltown, Dauphin County, Pennsylvanien, Amerika. Die Zeugen waren das Ehepaar u. der ehrw. herr Pfarrer Waldensius.

Mein lieber Gott
ich danke Dir
Wenn Du nicht bist
wär ich nicht hier.

Lisa and Lotte's Birth and Baptismal Certificates, written in German as it was customary among the German settlers in the Pennsylvania regions.

23215
NORTON PUBLIC LIBRARY
101 E. LINCOLN
NORTON, KANSAS 67654

About this Story

The Swiss and Germans who came to live in Pennsylvania in the seventeenth and eighteenth centuries were called Pennsylvania Dutch because they spoke *Deutsch,* or German. Most of them were Protestants (Moravians, Mennonites, Amish, Schwenkfelders, etc.) who, because of their religion, had been persecuted in Europe. In America, many of them became happy, prosperous farmers—just like the Schimmelpfennigs in this story.

Rudi and the Distelfink should be imagined to be taking place in Pennsylvania, somewhere near Lancaster, in the 1820's or 1830's, well before the railroads were built. For back in those days, the Conestoga wagons (first built in the eighteenth century along Conestoga Creek, just outside of Lancaster) were all-important for hauling freight and produce from the mountainous back country, down to York, Harrisburg, Lancaster, Philadelphia, and back. And the powerful teamsters who drove them—like Willi Stolzfuss— were some of the most highly-paid workmen of the era.

As for the distelfink himself, it is the bird we now call the goldfinch, but which used to be called the "thistle bird," because it loves to feed on thistle seeds.

Many huge stone barns, painted with decorative hex signs, were built by the Pennsylvania Dutch. They are still to be seen in many places in Pennsylvania. Their characteristic farm buildings, as well as the folkways, designs, recipes, and traditions of the Pennsylvania Dutch, have left a permanent stamp on American life.